Isabel
clark

LITTLE RED RIDING HOOD

Retold by Heather Amery
Illustrated by Stephen Cartwright

Language Consultant: Betty Root
There is a little yellow duck to find on every page.

TIGER BOOKS INTERNATIONAL

Once upon a time, there was a little girl who lived with her mother on the edge of a big, dark forest. The little girl's Grandmother made her a bright red cloak with a hood. She was so pleased with it, she wore it whenever she went out, so everyone called her Little Red Riding Hood.

One day, her mother called Little Red Riding Hood into the kitchen.

"Your Grandmother is ill," she said. "I've put some food in a basket and you can take it to her. Go along the path to her cottage but, remember, don't talk to any strangers you meet on the way."

Little Red Riding Hood waved goodbye to her mother and went into the forest with the basket.

It was such a lovely sunny day, she sang a little song to herself as she skipped along the path. She did not see a big grey Wolf with gleaming eyes watching her from behind a tree.

Suddenly the Wolf jumped out in front of her. Little Red Riding Hood was frightened but the Wolf smiled at her.

"Where are you going, little girl?" he asked.

"I'm taking this basket of food to my Granny who lives in a cottage in the forest," she said.

The Wolf licked his lips and smiled.

"Why not pick some flowers for her?" he said.

Little Red Riding Hood did not like the Wolf's smile but she knew her Grandmother would like the flowers.

"That's a good idea, Mr Wolf," she said, politely.

She put down her basket and started to pick a big bunch of flowers. The Wolf watched her for a moment and smiled again, showing all his sharp white teeth. Then he ran silently down the path through the forest to find Grandmother's cottage. He was very, very hungry.

The Wolf found the cottage and looked through the window. Grandmother was sitting up in bed.

He knocked loudly on the front door.
"Come in," called Grandmother.
The Wolf opened the door and ran in. Quick as a flash, he gobbled her up in one great gulp.

Then he climbed slowly into Grandmother's bed and put on her night cap and glasses. He pulled the bed clothes right up to his chin and settled down on the pillows.

"Little Red Riding Hood will soon be here," he said to himself, and waited for her to come in.

When Little Red Riding Hood reached the cottage with her basket of food and bunch of flowers, she knocked on the door.

"It's me, Granny," she said.

"Come in, my dear," called the Wolf in a squeaky voice. "I'm in my bedroom."

Little Red Riding Hood opened the door.
"Hello Granny," she said. "I've brought you
some food and flowers." Then she stared and
stared. "But, Granny," she said, "what big eyes
you have."

"All the better to see you with," said the Wolf.

"But, Granny," said Little Red Riding Hood, feeling a little frightened, "what big ears you have."

"All the better to hear you with," said the Wolf, smiling at her.

"But, Granny," said Little Red Riding Hood, feeling very frightened, "what big teeth you have."

"All the better to eat you with," growled the Wolf, and he jumped out of bed.

Little Red Riding Hood screamed, but the Wolf gobbled her up in one great gulp. Then he climbed slowly back into bed, pulled up the bedclothes, yawned loudly and fell asleep.

Out in the forest, a Woodman heard the scream. "I wonder what that was," he said. "I'd better go and see if the old lady is all right."

He ran as fast as he could to the cottage, rushed in through the open door and straight into Grandmother's bedroom.

When he saw the Wolf asleep in Grandmother's bed, he killed it with one mighty blow of his axe. Then he cut it open with his knife.

Inside were Little Red Riding Hood and her Grandmother, a little squashed and crumpled, but alive and very happy to be rescued.

"Thank you very much for saving us from the wicked Wolf," said Grandmother. "Now he can never frighten anyone ever again."

The Woodman dragged the dead Wolf out of the cottage and they all sat down to a delicious meal.

First published in 1981 by Usborne Publishing Ltd, 83-85 Saffron Hill, London, EC1N 8RT, England. Copyright © 1992, 1988 Usborne Publishing Ltd.

This edition published in 1997 by Tiger Books International PLC, Twickenham. ISBN 1-85501-964-7